DATE DUE

UPI 261-2

The Sandwoman

Prose Series 8

Madeleine
Ouellette-Michalska

The Sandwoman

Short Stories

Translated by
Luise von Flotow

Guernica
Montreal, 1990

Original title: *La femme de sable*
Copyright © 1987 Éditions de l'Hexagone and Madeleine Ouellette-
Michalska.
Translation © 1990 Guernica Editions, Inc. and Luise von Flotow.
All rights reserved.
Printed in Canada.

Antonio D'Alfonso
Guernica Editions Inc.
P.O. Box 633, Station N.D.G.
Montréal (Québec), Canada H4A 3R1

The Publisher and the Translator gratefully acknowledge financial
assistance from The Canada Council and Le ministère des Affaires
culturelles du Québec.

Legal Deposit — second Quarter
Bibliothèque nationale du Québec and National Library of Canada.

Canadian Cataloguing in Publication Data
Ouellette-Michalska, Madeleine, 1935-
[Femme de sable. English]
The sandwoman
(Prose series ; 8)
Translation of: La femme de sable.
ISBN 0-920717-24-1

I. Title. II. Title: Femme de sable. English. III. Series.
PS8579.U44F413 1990 C843'.54 C90-090075-X
PQ3919.2.O84F413 1990

Contents

The Sandwoman

The triangle of sun caught in the crook of his folded arm was streaked with shadow. At that same moment, the sound of footsteps in the sand vibrated in his ears. He slowly slanted his head in order not to blur the ray of light fastened to his forehead. The sky rolled above him. He rubbed his eyelids. Each time he moved, he felt the same bursting of burning stone along his temples.

Flat on his belly, Karim cleaved to the earth and let it devour him. The world upside down was quite pleasant. He forgot the tricks of incoherence that could be played on him if he stretched out his arm or puffed out his chest to sit up. He would detach himself from this somnolence and put things back in their place when he felt like it. He would get up, and the ground would flatten out under his feet, brushing only the edges of the distant sky.

Footsteps continued to stir the sand near him. He moistened his lips with saliva. God, it was hot, and this grainy crumbly matter at his temples made him thirsty! He felt for his gourd and found it empty. He could no longer postpone the effort required to get up. He began by bending one leg, but the moment he braced his back, something cracked through the length of his spinal column. The earth's axis swayed. He pushed his hands into the ground and raised his shoulders, curving his back into the position of a cobra. The bone of the planet was missing. He felt himself slip into empty space. He quickly clutched his gourd, willing the drop into hell not to happen. The comedy of death would not be played for him yet. It was amply enough to be born and to die once.

He arched his back firmly and pushed away the serpent's bite. With a leap, he was up. The race across fiery rails began. He ran, finally stopped. Then sat down and calmly opened his eyes.

A few steps away, a woman was asleep, snoring almost. He wanted to wake her up and warn her of the dangers that threatened her, but he changed his mind. She was beautiful. The serpent would never dare to approach her. She must be strong to challenge the sun this way. Her even breathing swelled her breasts and rounded her belly over the edge of the bikini that circled her sex. This woman was afraid of nothing. Or else she would never have dared flaunt herself like this on a beach invaded by spellbound males.

Was it three o'clock when he left the main café in town? It did not matter. Time was an invention of men. Beyond them was the sun, a magic god, the great and terrifying sparrowhawk that hunted down life and harried it maliciously. He heard himself burst into laughter. Fortunately, it did not wake up the woman. She remained asleep, her flaming hair tossed to one side of her face.

He stretched out his arm to touch her, but felt he could not reach her. She moved away as he approached. Was she possessed by the devil, or did he not have the nerve? He called out two or three names which she appeared not to hear, and concluded her name was not Judith, or Christine, or Rachel. He would have liked her name to be Christine, yet it was not really necessary. She could just as well have no name at all.

The man knelt down in the sand, at a slight distance from the woman, in the narrow basin where the tide was beginning to cover the shore. He turned his back to the waves and carefully traced a curved line on the ground. Hesitantly, he traced a second line after the first, measuring with his arm the distance that separated this one from the other, and then began digging around these edges. When he was satisfied with the developing relief, he completed the rudimentary shapes with an oval lightly inclined to the right.

The head grew with each moment. Disregarding the facial traits, he moved on, concerned only with attaching it to the throat he was shaping with care. His hands slipped gently along the curves and fashioned the breasts that he wanted firm, ripe, high. He massaged them in a circular motion that softened at the point of the cones and lingered at the nipple. Pulsations warmed his wrists. He was sure he would never be cured of the desire he felt for women, and he gave in to this madness like a fragile pleasure.

He pushed his arms deeper and deeper into the womb of the warm earth. He raped the sand to slake the instinct that impelled him toward the female, the eternal woman, wife of the great hawk who reigned on high and was biting the nape of his neck. He covered his shoulders with his towel and began tapering an arm that he copied from the sleeping woman's. Then he shaped the other and leaned forward to examine his work. His eyes travelled from the real woman to the sandwoman. From the one he took the feeling that he wanted to share with the other before the sun started slipping away beyond the line of the eucalyptus that edged the shore.

The tide was still rising. He felt it approach in flat waves that rolled cones of shells onto the shingle before they spread out across the beach. A moment of silence lay between two murmurs of foam, and then the water siphoned off the sand packed between his legs. He was not worried about the continual decrease in elevation that was beginning to separate him from his sculpture. He was sure the sea would leave him time to complete his work.

He rounded out generous hips that opened to the sun, and had the impression that the whole of life could rest there. In the hollows of flesh he imagined a secret haven where he could lull himself after his ecstasy. His hand fashioned a protrusion below the abdomen. The mound of Venus rose there, fragile, at the summit of a pink bulge. Two lips gaped open under his closed fist. Violently, he embraced this moaning, half-conscious woman, whose hair was spread out in the sun's flamboyance. He emptied himself into her, and plunged her into the sea. A few minutes passed, and she reappeared, dazzling, transfigured.

He kissed her and she smiled at him in silence. The sun had sunk down considerably. Driven off by the tide, it was setting behind the crest of the eucalyptus. A wave touched the legs of the woman stretched out on the sand. She opened her eyes, looked at the sea, touched her forehead and her mouth. Then she got up, brushed the sand off her skin and picked up her scattered clothing.

Did he actually speak to her? Did he ask her whether she lived in town, and did he really offer to drive her home? He remembered nothing. He only recalled offering her a drink although he knew his gourd was empty. He insisted, and she raised absent eyes replying: " I don't know you."

He tried to explain that he knew her well. She shrugged her shoulders and adjusted the belt of her dress in silence. She brushed her hair, stepped into her espadrilles and took the bag he handed her. He waited in vain for a word of thanks. She took the path that edged the beach without looking back. He saw her walk, luminous against the tufts of mimosa that

lined the bay she was circling. To detain her he
ran to pick a flower for her, but his gesture got
no response.

A heavy wave crashed onto the shore and
covered the woman, erasing her hands, and
soon her arms and shoulders. The sun was only
a narrow band on the horizon. Another wave
came in aid of the first, and the sandwoman
disappeared, carried off by the violence of the
tide. At the spot where she had rested, there
was nothing left except a vague alluvion soon
devoured by the sea's backwash.

Someone burst out laughing behind Karim.
He turned, ready to lash out. He looked, but
found no one. The beach had emptied. Between two eucalyptus roots, a serpent was
eyeing him, gleaming like a blade.

The Terrace of the Belvedere

1
My Sweet Lord

The man rolled over in bed and was surprised
to hit his head against the music.

He ran his hand over the roughcast wall and
felt it welling out of the cold plaster. He opened
his eyes to see it coming out of the sweat-dren-
ched mattress, the half-open closet, the neon
tube that lit up the mirror above the washbasin.
It was flowing in from everywhere, driven by
the beat of the drums and brass, hurling into
the shutter slats, where it merged with muffled
noises and distant barking.

He sat up and made a trellis of his fingers
across his face to protect himself from flies
swirling under his nose before they tangled in
the damp hairs on his chest and arms. He tried
to catch one, but it escaped. Exasperated, he let
his hands drop onto the bolster and remained
motionless, listening to the diffuse roar of the
nearby sea. The mosquitoes' buzzing grew
louder and louder. He knew he would not be
able to get to sleep again.

He struck a match. The white shape stretched out beside him moved. He followed the
curved lines of the warm flesh slipping away

from him. Though tempted to clasp and hold it back, he decided not to touch it. His sleeping wife always frightened him a little. In slumber, she embraced the void, her gaze turned toward a shadow world that excluded him.

"Don't get up first," she had begged before going to bed. She was so afraid of the dark, she wanted to keep him near until dawn, that reassuring moment when she could do without him. When it arrived, she would wrench herself from his embrace, wash and perfume herself, and make her hair froth about her shoulders. She would draw herself up before him, secret, elusive, always ready to rear up. In spite of his wish to subjugate her, he never managed to possess her totally.

Behind the guest rooms, the orchestra was playing *My Sweet Lord*. In the ballroom she was dancing frenetically. With her tunic wound about her, she undulated around the supporting torso, displaying herself to the males who devoured her with their eyes. And that he could not stand. He could have smashed their faces, and slapped hers, for refusing to admit what he constantly repeated: you do not offer your body to men who are expecting just that.

She would reproach him for his obsession, assuring him that dancing was an innocent pleasure for her and, for his information, if he refused to escort her, she would go dancing anyway. Slumped in his chair, he would turn his back to the dance floor and sip the smuggled cognac he had paid the earth for, but which would not ignite when he spilt some on a paper napkin. He was obviously being cheated. He hated being cheated.

This evening, he had resisted all her pleas and had only had two slow dances with her. He did not understand this passion for a pleasure that left him cold. He liked only classical music. Besides, he found physical exertion repellent. Movement exhausted him without bringing him any of the elation she talked about. In his opinion, the rhythm, the orchestrated repetition of the same theme or motif, was tiring enough in itself.

The man plugged his ears to block out *My Sweet Lord*. Finding this impossible, he leaned over his sleeping wife and examined her throat, the swelling of her breast under her nightdress, her arms alongside her body. Bit by bit, he saw her disappear into the foam of the sheets, her legs open, one hand raised above her head. She was drifting off and he could not stop her. A few air bubbles rose from her pale mouth. He suppressed a cry. He had to rush to the beach and save her while there was still time.

He ran out of the room, skirting the dance hall where steamy couples were languishing. He almost tripped on the step separating the patio from the staircase that led down to the sea. "*My Sweet Lord*," he implored finally reaching the path that fell sharply down the cliff. The vision of the white body lying in the swells pursued him. He saw it slowly sink down, rise again to the surface of the troubled waters, and then flow toward the concentric circle which swallowed up the sea, sucking it in with a great soughing eddy.

He was sorry he had abandoned Barbara in the middle of the dance floor when the jerk suddenly began to shake the bodies and knock them into each other. When he had seen his wife's hips seize the distortion that had begun in her chest, then grind it in the depths of her belly and release it with a short sharp movement of the loins, he had said: "I can't take it anymore" — and had abruptly left her.

He had downed two or three cognacs and angrily finished his cigarette. The dance hall had misted over. He had gotten up, jostled a few dancers and pushed aside the gawkers gathered at the edge. The moon came to a rest above his head and guided him toward the sea. He looked for the Great Bear in the tangle of stars attached to its forehead. He could not find it and gave up trying to find the North Star as well.

The only thing that mattered now was this hurried descent, this desire to force his way through the space that floated between gorse bushes and tufts of cactus. The path narrowed. At the edge of a slope, he felt someone breathing nearby. A shape loomed up, blocking his path. He said: "Excuse me," politely making way. It came closer. He touched the ground to make sure he was not dreaming.

His hand groped through the rough grass, up the length of a sturdy tibia, around a slender joint. He said again: "Excuse me," and moved on a few steps. Two cold eyes stared at him. He stopped to catch his breath. The shape moved, and a mane tangled in his hand. He shouted: "Hey!" — and the animal moved off.

Young goats came skipping underfoot. If he had not been in such a hurry to reach the shore, he would have picked them up and fondled them. He would have let them frisk about the bed and enjoyed watching them, his shoulders resting on the foam bolster which he had folded under his head to see them better. Barbara resembled them when she danced. She was graceful and light, almost diaphanous. Because she was his wife, he could not stand this transparence she offered to the lust of any man that snatched at it.

He liked her better asleep, innocent as a child. Heavy with sleep, she would rest at his side, warm and soft. He need only slide his hand under her nightdress and cup one breast in the hollow of his hand to feel her all hot and moaning with pleasure. She seemed able to find her balance in the depth of the night into which she sank, mysterious and pale, her hair undone, her clear profile lit by the crescent moon shining through the lowered blinds. When he saw her like that, he wanted to take her far away to a desert island where he would be the only one to approach her.

He caught sight of the island sailing far out between two lemon trees: tiny, hardly longer than the bed. Three big steps would take him around it, and he would always be able to find the spot where Barbara hid on the days she closed herself off in silence, her cheeks splotched with tears. At the age of thirty-five, he still did not understand why women cried. On the island it would be windy. Tears would dry before he had a chance to notice them.

He stopped a moment to catch his breath and inhale the air rising from the open sea. The night stretched out before his eyes like a devouring womb. Studded with stars, it absorbed the beach, the fishing boats moored at the shore, the villas that dotted the coast. It swallowed up the universe in a hazy lapping sound that wrinkled the water's surface, where frogs were tearing one another to pieces. The flat stone steps around Sidi Rachid's kiosk slipped by under his feet. He rounded the chairs piled under the arbour and followed the row of tables lined up below the canvas cover pierced by the face of the moon which now called him.

His hand brushed a leg stretched out at his height. Two human forms were copulating beside him, a black shape wrapped around a white shape and trying to hold it in its grip. The two-fold breathing swelled, mingled with the sounds of the coast, and finally trickled into the rattle of an exhausted animal. The bodies collapsed. Two consenting souls fell to the bottom of an abyss. Their arms now dangled over each side of the table like eucalyptus branches torn in a storm.

The man took off his espadrilles to muffle his steps and went on. He moved across the warm sand without looking back, pushing the soles of his feet into the grainy flesh that closed on his heels giving him a feeling of well-being that he savoured voluptuously. There was no wind. The air was dry. Cracks of heat splintered off the stones that children had collected into barely visible piles. Things had lost their shape, their texture. They were melting into a milky continuity that cradled the seven continents in brotherhood.

This land was like Barbara. It only gave way at night. In an attempt to tame it, he had forced himself to discover its customs. He had read its literature, listened to its music, frequented its cafés. He had wandered through its casbahs and heard the muezzin issue his appeals five times a day from the top of a minaret. He had enjoyed the shows of belly-dancing, stuffed himself with couscous and chorba, kebabs and honey-cakes. He had commiserated on their days of fasting, their rituals, their nightly orgies, and had even gotten himself invited to a wedding where he had been bold enough to kiss the bride.

In an honest attempt, he had forced himself to see everything, grasp everything, understand everything. And then, one fine day, for no reason, he had had enough. He had developed an aversion for the streets teeming with lone men, the sluggishness of the administration, the stench of certain neighbourhoods. He had gotten tired of signing forms and filling out papers. He had even gotten tired of the smell of coffee. So he had gone back to wine — whisky and cognac whenever possible — and stopped playing tourist. From that moment on, he had no longer worried about hiding his racism. He had even become quite proud of it, returning to initial truths that he realised he had mistakenly rejected for exotic novelties.

On the beach, however, this old state of grace returned. While he flattened the tiny dunes with his feet and watched the rings of dust spiral around his ankles, his weariness and resentment drained away, and he began to like humanity, making no distinction for language, race or colour. As his liberal beliefs came back to him, he regretted not having explored enough of this country in which he had come to live. The scent of mimosa wafted toward him, and he felt gusts of understanding for this strange people that he had not known how to like.

Forgetting his pain, he imbibed the peace of the night. The silence and solitude purified him. Barbara was asleep, and he was far away from the poverty that swilled in the adobe huts clinging to the mountain beyond the cliff road. He cast off his worries about healing the sick and feeding the starving. The clear air purified him, liberating him from all his illusory challenges.

A rock closed off the bay into which he had ventured. He carefully followed the ribbon of sand around the lagoon that the sea had cast into a circular dip at the end of the inlet. He tossed his espadrilles over his shoulder. Then, hesitating a moment, he made a jerky half-turn. He had begun humming *My Sweet Lord*. Unwittingly, he was trying the dance steps he had always refused to learn. He straightened up and rapidly hit his left foot against his right, as he had seen it done a few hours earlier. Bending forward, he raised his arms and watched an imaginary partner twirl around. Barbara was turning in front of him, skillfully displaying her charms. She rolled her hips in a movement that rose to her breasts, made her throat tremble and her shoulders quiver. He suddenly wanted to hug her to him.

Barbara, this woman more beautiful than all the others, was asleep in the hollow of the waves, rocked by its swells. He had to get to her and tear her away from the sea. He moved toward the water, waded in to his waist and dived into dull green reflections that splattered his body. He was swimming, following the luminous trail that drew him on ever more quickly, unaware of the fatigue weighing him down. With hands outstretched, he clung to the undulating comet that linked his shoulders to the rock he was nearing.

Finally he touched the sandy shore. Barbara was waiting for him on the island, her head tipped back, ready to receive him. He smoothed her hair and devoured her lips. He consented to the madness that recreated their bodies. He made love to her in harmony with this land that had brought them together, which let them discover the desert dust and the parched rivers. He recognised the scent of jasmine emanating from her, the perfume of asphodel, the moist nights tempered with sweetness. Barbara was his oasis. He pressed her to him, and her pallor merged with the moon's.

A lapping rippled the water. He raised his head and saw a small boat glide onto the sand behind him. A stranger got out, wrapped in a burnous which concealed a long shape vaguely resting in the crook of his arms. He approached with difficulty, pulling his feet from the ebb of the waves that rolled sand onto the shore, only to take it up again and return it to the sea. The burnous fell to the ground in an arc. A wreck slipped from the open robe and dropped to the ground in front of the black legs that cut through the halo flowing around the rock that seemed to be floating in the mirages. The stranger waited, impassive, before the inert body on the ground.

The man approached and examined the hair spread out under the crescent moon. He gazed at the open mouth, the livid colouring, the flat breasts, her hips which narrowed into a silken stream and flowed toward the waves. A cry rose from the open sea. This call made him stumble over the woman. He saw that she was looking at him through half-open eyes, asking to be kissed.

He threw himself upon her, licked the salt from her skin, breathed on her forehead, her throat, her shoulders. A gentle sea covered them. Algae mingled with their hair, and tufts of seaweed filled their mouths. They grew, climbed the rocky ledge, and scrambled down the cliff, covered with stars. Their spines gave way. They collapsed, unable to get up.

"*Hemchi*!" cried the stranger from the boat. He began to beat them. They got up and fled, their backs turned to the Great Bear who was laughing at them. A young goat ran with them, and soon outstripped them and stopped before a mimosa bush where they sank down, half-dead. They were happy to rediscover the security of the warm earth, its smell of parched grass. Barking sounds rose in the distance. The man pushed aside the branches that blocked his view. Below, whitings leapt on the shell of the smooth water. High above them, lights blinked from the windows of the Belvedere.

Barbara touched his cheek laughing: "You big lump, you really did have too much to drink. You gave me a fright. Lie down and try to sleep."

2

The Vikings

Lakhdar entered dragging his feet, and took a seat in his usual place at the edge of the dance floor, behind a column at the third table.

From there he could eye the incoming women at his leisure. Most of them he knew, and classified them by what they had already allowed or refused him. This predictable book-keeping bored him. He dreamt of decisive assaults, struggles conducted according to rigorous and implacable strategies, and awaited the arrival of new prey.

These wives of technicians or lesser civil servants were quite different from the colonial aristocracy who remained hidden in their villas day and night. Deliberately casual, they changed dresses like handkerchiefs, drank and smoked. He watched them pass by, and at the resurgence of old desires recognised the ones that had already moved him. Eyes closed he could reconstitute for each one the hollow of her back, the shape of her hips, the outline of her chest or the round form of her breasts.

He watched them evolve, and remembered the indolent ones he had taken the pleasure to animate, the light ones he had swung with to rock music, the clumsy ones he had had to tow around in a slow dance. They all belonged to the *Roumie* clan, this race of platinum-blondes that awakened exotic visions in him. They represented the easy life: travel, freedom, all the things of which he had been deprived for a long time. Instinctively he pushed brunettes out of his lust range. Beneath their sensual ardour, he had often felt their irresistible need to attach themselves to him through marriage or a lasting relationship.

"Heh!" Jimmy, a large Saint-Bernard, part Belgian, part German, clapped him on the shoulder. In his inevitable khaki jacket he often trespassed on his territory, but had an agreeable temperament and readily paid the check. Stretching his long legs out under the table, he sniffed out the crowd.

"Anything new?"

"All old goods."

"What about the little one over there?"

"The red head in the nightdress? She looks dumb."

Lakhdar felt the Saint-Bernard's disapproval. He was often reproached for being unfair to his countrywomen. He could not say why he tended to reject them. When they were educated, they aped European women. When they were not, they earned their living as bar girls and frequented these places, waiting till evening to unfold the bats' wings, dully flattened down under the veil during the day. Either way they represented the past or the future. He wanted no attachment, no country. The dark hole of birth led to the equally frightening hole of death. His attempt to make this journey as pleasant as possible took the place of any plan or occupation.

The big Saint-Bernard clicked his tongue, indicating the people coming in. There were four of them, the women preceding the men as in an official procession. The scene took on aspects of a cortege. Two women, tall and majestic, looked the guests over. One of them was fitted into a pair of white pants overhung with a scarlet tunic. The other undulated in the folds of a long gathered skirt. Were they descended from a long line of aristocrats? They projected the scandalous splendour of the illustrated history book his teacher had allowed him to leaf through at school. Lakhdar looked at the cardboard cones around the lightbulbs fixed on the ceiling and, for the first time, the lighting seemed pitiful.

The couples took the next table. He could examine the women at leisure. The first one had shining hair, a loud voice, a well-tucked waistline. She moved her long lacquered hands over the table while she talked, displacing objects that swayed under her influence. She had dark eyes and her aquiline nose dominated the rest of her profile. Generous hips and a sparkling laugh attenuated her rather virile build. Lakhdar heard her name was Geneviève. It hardly suited her.

The other woman was slimmer and seemed almost fragile. She had a high forehead, a sensual mouth, a long neck hidden by abundant hair. Her gestures were restrained, but her active gaze belied the placid appearance. This moderate body, which seemed too perfect, did not attract Lakhdar. She had the cold distinction of a Countess. He could have looked at her for hours without daring to propose what he had in mind.

"Do you want the Amazon or the Countess?"

"Give me a minute."

The big Saint-Bernard scented the warm flesh of the two women and stroked his moustache. He had not seen any as tall and handsome for a long time. Lakhdar watched him cross his long legs, sure that this beast was convinced of his Nordic race's superiority. He would have liked to slam a right hook straight into his jaw, had he not been afraid of getting stuck paying the bill at the Minaret where they were supposed to have lunch together the next day.

The women were on the dance floor, in the process of taming the jerk that had begun. The Amazon tried to copy the Countess' moves, attempting to reproduce the thrust of breasts meant to absorb the abrupt release of the hips. She was not very successful; her belly failed to return the impulse that crossed it. Her arms and legs flailed out from her body, in contrast to the Countess' which stayed close to their center of gravity.

The husbands seemed disconcerted by the scrutiny to which they were subject. They began to carefully study the drinks list brought by the waiter. This gave Lakhdar the chance to examine their blonde heads, their red beards, their faintly visible lashes. One was more pale than the other, his shoulders were lower and he had less hair. But they resembled each other like two brothers, and both seemed to be equally self-conscious about the impression they were making. Lakhdar found this embarrassment justified. Their people had allowed women to do what they wanted for centuries. The time had come to pay the price. Performing the belly dance did not compromise a woman's reputation. It was part of the tradition and respected the laws of calculated seduction which would lead to festivities consecrated by marriage. It had nothing in common with these modern contortions unsanctioned by any sacrament.

The two men got up. They lifted the women out of the last shakes of the jerk and slid them into a slow dance gently suggested by the orchestra. Quiet, almost somnolent, they leaned on the proffered shoulders, abandoning their docile bodies to the indifferent hands caressing them. A streak of lightning lit the windows of the Belvedere. The sea invaded the room, suddenly turning it blue. Branches over the open arches, above each window, bent under the force of the wind. Fresh air swept over the tables. Lakhdar ordered two more beer, ceaselessly watching the women.

They had changed partners without modifying their behaviour in the least. The swaying bodies, hardly affected by the new constellation of shapes, formed an alloy of nordic skins bronzed by the African sun. The men's legs were as stiff as their bodies were hard. Their ancestors had skimmed the seas and annexed land. They had never conquered rhythm.

A glass of cognac spilt on the next table. The big Saint-Bernard took advantage of this to take the Amazon off to a frenzied cha-cha-cha. In the knowledge that he excelled in this dance, he counted on his skill to eliminate the competition. His feet tapped the floor rapidly while his bent arms underscored each of the sustained moves. He fitted his steps to those of the woman whose hips no longer held back the horizontal flow which was being absorbed, blended and ejected by her thighs.

The reach of their movements increased constantly. The Belgian-German was exaggerating. Lakhdar decided he could not put up with this triumph any longer. He went over and bowed in front of the man he believed was the Countess' husband. The response was : "If she's not too tired." The Countess was not tired. She lifted her long skirt, ready to lead the way. Lakhdar led her to the centre of the dance floor. There was only one thing that bothered him. He would have to make conversation.

"Who are you?"

"No one."

"English?"

"God forbid."

" German?"

" No."

" American?"

" No."

He felt quite proud to have asked all these questions. Basically, he could not care less what she was. She was light, danced well enough and had a pretty smile. He continued, pushed by the desire to prove himself to the Saint-Bernard.

" Nordic, in any case."

" You're getting warm."

" Swedish?"

" Almost."

" Norwegian?"

" Right."

She laughed and he knew she was lying. She could just as well be French, Bulgarian, or even *Québécois*. Aid organisations sent them from everywhere. The West had become a reservoir of competence, wealth and beauty. The Middle East was still attractive for its mysticism, nonchalance, poverty. This exchange, due to climate, seemed natural to him.

" Have you been here long?"

" I just got here."

" Are you enjoying yourself?"

" Very much."

" What do you like?"

" Everything."

" Will you be staying long?"

" As long as necessary."

" What do you do?"

"I'm a spy. Zone 9-118. Sssh! Someone could be listening."

"What's your name?"

"Barbara."

With a finger on her lips, she was telling more and more lies. Lakhdar knew women did not spy on anything. Women put men into trances and then suddenly disappeared without a trace. Their lives were elsewhere. They could not bear walls and barred windows. They were made for the sun and fresh air.

When the Saint-Bernard returned his partner to the table of *Roumies*, Lakhdar felt he could do the same. He led the Countess back and waited long enough for an invitation to join them, taking care to show he was pleased. He always distrusted foreigners. Either they admitted their racist feelings and their frankness was unbearable, or they played the diplomat and became condescending. Both attitudes annoyed him profoundly; he made it his duty to re-establish justice by taking their wives.

The Amazon made an effort to put him at his ease. She raised her glass and said: "Cheers!" He raised his. The conversation turned to his origins. They thought that by seeing Mediterranean blood in him — Spanish or Italian ancestors — they would be flattering him. At most, they could detect Kabyle ancestry, an attachment to the Mediterranean, the great river that separates Europe and Africa, as they had learnt in elementary school. To please them, he said he had been born in the mountains and had never lived in the city. The Countess even discovered Indian features in him. He replied: "I did my military service in Mexico."

She continued: "I thought I'd met you somewhere before."

"That was in the Yucatan", he said, "I was killing iguanas, and you were chasing butterflies."

They were all a little drunk and laughed noisily. If he had said he was Chinese, they would not have questioned it, their mood was so open. In the belief that his efforts should be compensated, he asked the Amazon to dance, having first made a deep bow to her husband. In the beginning he always asked the husband's permission before he laid a finger on the wife. It was only later when he embraced her completely that he broke with this point of etiquette.

In his arms she did not seem as tall as before. Lakhdar attributed this to his own merits and felt proud that he must be taller than the two Vikings. He stuck out his chest without completely straightening out his bowed shoulders. Listening to women guess his age always amused him. They would get lost in daring conjectures, be thrown off by his sideburns streaked with gray, come back to his moustache, his worldly eyes and, finally, admit they had to give up. He would ask them to name a figure for his pleasure. Their refusal would make him insist. He would say twenty-five, if they looked around forty. When they were nearer twenty, he would add on ten or fifteen years. This one admitted having two adolescent children. He appreciated her candour and told himself that for once he would not have to lie.

" I don't know how to dance."

" That doesn't matter."

For the moment, it was not important at all. He saw she was surprised to have been selected, and took care to fit her steps to his. She confessed she had not danced in a long time and was afraid she was clumsy. He avoided excessive displays of skill, acrobatics and daring moves. He led her, looking straight into her eyes. She laughed simply. Perhaps with her, an adventure might be possible without too much fuss. He felt her strength and found it stimulating. She would not be in raptures right after the first dance. He would have to break down her resistance, make progress little by little.

He pressed her right hand gently. She did not respond. Her puritan education probably made her feign indifference. He could feel her body was hot under the tunic. Instinct advised him not to give up this woman. She would give in to him one day, and the roles would be reversed. Then he would refuse to be caught and would demand she learn how to dance perfectly. She would wear herself out following him, begging for his caresses and his vows. He would be deaf, and finally feel avenged.

The child of a poor family, he despised begging. In the casbah, filthy children stalked the Roumies who came in search of goatskins, Berber chests, trays and antique jewelry. Like flies sticking to honey, they would push out tattered hands and hold them suspended in the dust for hours. "*Kench maïnoub labi.*" The Roumies would pass by, blind to the out-stretched hands. Lakhdar could not bear the poverty inlaid on grimy doorways in alleys the sun never entered. Footsteps slipped over the paving stones. A wallet was stolen. Someone was shouting: "Stop! Thief!" In the stifling heat of the displays, a woman screamed her fear at faces of stone.

As a child, with his friends, Lakhdar often left the town and headed to the cliff road. They scaled the precipice and looked at the arches of the main square drop down to the sea where the terraces of the main street also disappeared. Then they reached the mountain. Blinded by the light, they made for clearings where scorpions swarmed beneath extremely heavy apricot-coloured stones. They reduced the beasts to impotence, and tying their tails together with string in the shape of a rosary took them to the edge of the road and threw at foreign cars. At first relieved not to have been hit by stones, the passengers then rolled up their windows with loud shrieks.

The fellah sons begged them to give up this game. They were just as cruel, but more timid than the town children, and recounted terrifying stories of reprisals to which their people had been subject. The group was persuaded and returned to the clearing, to hunt thrushes. They were masters of a subtle method — bewitching the bird by flashing lemon tree leaves before its eyes. The thrushes would freeze. Then the boys would down them with a blow on the breast, collect the fallen birds, run them, still hot and twitching, onto spits and roast them over a fire of dry roots.

Lakhdar gazed at the Amazon's breasts and sensed the moment when he would touch her below the left one, on the ribs which the jerk was knocking together beneath her tunic. The orchestra syncopated a harmony in brass, breaking the theme into muted variations that slid gently toward a suppression of rhythm. The drum banged out a few beats. The Amazon was no longer dancing. Lost in the jolts of a beat she could not follow any more, she mopped her forehead and protested: " They're totally crazy!" She was panting, out of breath, amazed at the marvels she had accomplished.

A slow dance was beginning and he knew its power. He encircled her waist. She seemed inclined to let herself be led. The warm voice of Brahim always softened women up. He was the irresistibly perverse villain whose saviour they hoped to become. But the melody would continue and reveal the dancers' sadness. They would lament their lost adolescence, their middle-class lives ridden with anxiety.

The Amazon would give way, like the others. He saw her resting her head on his shoulder, felt her body grow heavy against his.

As a child, he had once pillaged gardens, and often wished to gain access to a European house; now he was receiving this gift where he no longer asked for anything. He cajoled the woman who was sinking into his arms affecting unconsciousness. He took pleasure in brushing the hot thighs close to his. He forgot his bitterness and returned to essentials, the attraction of the male to the female, an eternal desire, indestructible, stronger than everything else.

"You're a heavenly dancer."

He heard the compliment and saw her stepping back from him, her gaze hidden behind trembling eyelids. She looked at him, impassive. He understood that he needed to move back and relax his embrace. The Amazon had suddenly become an impenetrable fortress. She was laughing, apparently forgetting what had passed between them. He remembered, and intended to remind her on the occasion of another dance.

The other husband had led the Countess onto the dance floor and was pressing her to him. If he had been married, Lakhdar would never have allowed another man to come near his wife. Love was not a consideration in this conviction based on honour, one of the few points on which he could still agree with his family. After they had returned to their table, the Amazon made a fan from a triangle of paper torn out of the tablecloth, and began fanning herself, her fake bracelets clinking. This movement of air revived the sugary scent he had breathed during the dance. Again he wanted her.

Suddenly she stopped her movement to find the source of the gaze she could feel riveted on her neck. She turned around. Two eyes were set on her.

"Who is that guy behind us?"

"My uncle."

"You take your family dancing?"

"He followed me because I went out without telling him."

"You still have to ask for permission to go out?"

"Here you're never an adult while there is still a father."

"But he's not your father."

"It's the same thing."

The Amazon's laugh ripped open the silence. Her husband lowered his eyes and an ironic smile crossed his face. He was hearing a truth he found pleasing. The Belgian-German detested discussions. In a conciliatory gesture, he offered cigarettes to Lakhdar and the friend who now proclaimed: "I'm a racist, and I like to say so every time I get the chance." A great thrust of the chin accompanied this pitiful assertion. Racism was a fact on both sides; why bother confessing.

A waltz was beginning. Lakhdar headed to the dance floor with the Amazon on his arm.

"Don't pay any attention. He can't possibly believe what he says."

"The contempt is about equal on both sides, you know."

"He's been drinking."

"Don't worry about defending him. I'm used to it."

Lakhdar had long measured the gap between them. On the one hand, there were big cars, villas, good food and regularly filled bank accounts. On the other hand, there were distraught months' ends, discomfort, poverty. It was enough to go to the souk and take in the smell of the burnous to realise that a hundred years of history separated them. It would have been insane to try to take this step in one day. Europe had taken its time growing old, and Lakhdar knew what the Arab world had contributed to it.

The Roumies' complacency had hurt Lakhdar for a long time, but he had cured himself of his sensitivity. Instead of taking part in their sterile debates, he was silent and slept with their wives. They did not lack self-importance either for that matter, but in general they were friendly. On their way to bed they would often take the blame for the defects of colonialism. Lakhdar salved their consciences and asked them to make love in silence. They let themselves be convinced and ended up abandoning themselves and forgetting the ravages of history.

A scarlet streak of lightning struck the sea. Bewitched, the Amazon gazed at the windows, repeating: "It's amazing!" He felt her vibrance, aroused by the dry storm and the demands of her body. He firmed his left hand and made her turn more quickly in order to dizzy her with the beat. He whirled her about under the light of the turning lamps. The light spread into thousands of kaleidoscopic pieces that caught in their steps. A sense of emptiness took them up little by little, leading them far away from the room and the bystanders, to a quiet place where the mind grew numb in the euphoria of fleshly satisfaction.

He twirled the woman, anticipating the approaching *dénouement*. To shorten the wait, he reduced the circles of the waltz. The orchestra accelerated the beat. She closed her eyes and began to tremble — feverish, overwrought. He caught her out of the dizziness that tossed her into the opposite direction, and embraced her violently. He held her pressed against him, trembling, while the dance floor continued to turn. Soon, she regained her balance, and was ready to succumb to new gravitational forces.

Lightning swept the sea from east to west, with ever clearer zigzags. The lights of the town moved out onto the water like fish drawn by the phosphorescent pier at the far edge of the shore. Orange streaks split the horizon lengthwise each time thunder rumbled. Lightning was ravaging the sky, and this woman was impervious to it. Devoured by an inner fire, she did not see the storm. Lakhdar watched her hanging at his neck and kissed the inner shell of her ear. He heard her moan with pleasure.

Brahim was wailing: "Don't let me go" — with the support of the orchestra pushing its heavy sensual harmonies in the background.

Afraid that he would not be able to wait much longer, Lakhdar began to caress her with precision. She swayed heavily with desire. She preceded him to the exit and he supported her, helping her make her way through the mass of men clustering around the orchestra. He thought he had crossed the line of obscenity and lust, when he saw a hand take hold of the woman's bare arm.

"May I caress hope?"

He recognised the patriarch and his obsequious voice. Uncle Ismael, the mosque rat, consumer of the sura and virgins, had spent three thousand dinars on his marriage to a sixteen year old girl he had tracked down in a secluded douar. That was more money than his land was worth. Six hectares of stones and thistles for a timid gazelle with superb eyes, whom he had deflowered in five minutes and now kept languishing behind closed shutters. The uncle's lecherous gaze was fixed on the Amazon, detailing her charms. She recognised him and stepped aside.

"Don't come near her or I'll kill you."

Lakhdar heard the sordid chortle. Lust burnt out of his rival's eyes. He recalled the patriarch's vicious tyranny, his torturous obsessions, his legendary hypocrisy, and suddenly he felt like cutting the umbilical cord that linked him to his clan. In the hope of making his

40

uncle's blood spurt before the Amazon's frightened eyes, he let the knife blade, tensed toward the old man's belly, cast its spell on him.

The steel shone in his hands. Calmly he advanced on the man who was backing away along the tables. The point of the knife would reach its goal. It was enough to follow its path. The movement would complete itself with a sudden lift of the right arm at the moment when his exasperation reached its height. Lakhdar made sure this moment did not come too soon. He had to let the incident absorb the audience's expectations, swell up with its delirium and fill out with its cries. He did not want an ordinary brawl conducted without honour or rules. The uncle was a scoundrel, but the family link imposed a duty he could not resist.

A streak of lightning swept over the audience, and seemed to strike the rock against which the Belvedere leaned. Under the blow, the drummer stopped beating the rhythm, leaving a few dancers frozen face to face. The Vikings, the Saint-Bernard, and the Countess rushed up in an attempt to join the Amazon surrounded by a mob of overly excited men.

Suddenly the doors of the hall opened. Police led off suspects. In a few minutes the room was empty, quiet, clean. Outside, shadows slipped down the stone staircase to the sea. A last car door slammed. Night returned to stagnate on the terrace. Hidden behind a disused pavillion, Lakhdar watched the Amazon run off in the direction of the guest rooms, followed by her escort. She ran, straight as an arrow, her burnous forming a dark trail behind her. He leapt onto the patio, picked up the knife left on the stone slabs, but she had disappeared into the dark. Alone, he raised his fist in her direction and shouted: "Dirty whore!"

The police car drove off. There was no one left to hear him.

3
Iris and Mimosa

Bachir straightened up and rubbed his back with his hand. There was no animal threatening him, yet he began to feel the bite of a strange pain. Eucalyptus branches could now entwine vine leaves, rams straddle goats. He was all alone. It was no use being a man.

At nineteen, he hardly knew anything about women. Cousins arrived in bunches and clustered in the dining room for funerals or weddings. A world of underarms furtively glimpsed through the openings of golden-edged gandouras, the dark line illuminating white breasts. Wild laughter veiled the doe's eyes they turned on him when he let his hand wander under their long skirts, let it slowly rise toward the moist and secret regions he eagerly explored, pushing the exacerbation of his desire always further — a torment this grim almond-scented fondling was never able to appease.

The crust was hard and dry between his teeth. Bachir regretted not being daring enough. He had seen the butter melting in the tagine but had not dared to dip his bread during the few seconds in which he heard the flies. The *maître d'hôtel*'s steps echoing on the slabs had neared the kitchens. Shouts and blows rained down on his hardened head. He escaped, whirling up the mosquitoes. Below his shirt the bread stuck to his skin, softening.

Grasshoppers brushed his temples. He caught one and flattened it against the wall. For some time he carefully watched the colour fade from olive to ochre, then grew tired of it and wondered how he would spend the afternoon. Herding goats and donkeys would mean moving and confronting the sun. The heat discouraged such an effort. Still he decided to get up. He might be lucky enough to find a car door open down on the parking lot. He tried them all but not a single one gave. The Roumies were becoming more and more wary, beginning to put everything they could not carry with them under lock and key.

The cars were asleep in the sun, crouched on their softened tires. He made the rounds several times, and tapped their burning bodies. The steel gave off a hollow sound. He returned to the guest house and lay down beside a wall, under the protection of a thorn hedge growing along a waterpipe. A little freshness rose from the dry earth. He crossed his hands and placed them quietly under the back of his neck. The guests must be having their siestas. He could allow himself a bit of a rest.

Comfortably settled, he forgot his cares and his masters. His body sank into the earth, and he felt good. To make sure he was not dreaming, he half-opened his eyes and watched the backs of the vine leaves move. Attached to the white wood trellises, they reached away from the wall and brushed against the eucalyptus branches leaning toward them. Leaves and branches intertwined. Bachir wondered whether plants, like men, had a body and a soul. "Only your soul will go to Paradise," said the Iman. "Your body will stay in the earth and be devoured by snakes and scorpions."

The Iman slapped anyone who moved about too much on the mats in the mosque. It was forbidden to laugh or twitch to chase off flies. Stiff in anxious torpor, the boys let the sweat run down their foreheads and waited for the old man to finish telling his terrifying stories. Always the same submersion in the Rummel, the flames of hell, the venomous bites, the race along fiery rails, thirst, darkness, emptiness. When the nightmare was over, the blue ceramic door would open onto the street setting them free, completely dizzy and as dazed as insects struck by too much light. They would grow used to the sun again and forget the clamour of the other world. Life would take them up once more. Struggles would recommence.

A man was approaching, and Bachir could tell without looking that it was a Roumie. They walked so heavily, so arrogantly. Bachir slipped along the wall and stretched his head forward. A white trouser cuff passed the threshold. He got up to go mechanically toward the guest house. In the corridor, a man stood waiting in front of number four with a bouquet of mimosa in his hand.

He did not know whether the man had knocked or was getting ready to. He remembered the blonde woman, a new guest to whom he had had to bring clean sheets in the morning, and who had demanded towels, a spray can of Vitox and a waste paper basket, a whole arsenal of luxury items the hotel did not have. He had promised some of it for the afternoon as he was required, and had tried to form a few sentences in French. She had been wearing a flowered dress, and during his painful attempts to express himself, he had tried to discern the shape of the body wrapped in the light fabric.

He hurried to a spot behind the wall of the room and glued an ear to the window edge. He heard nothing. He risked a glance through the blinds, and saw nothing either. He realised then that he would have to drive the sun from his retina. He batted his eyelids rapidly and was finally able to distinguish colours. The door was closing on the man as he moved toward the woman, speaking inaudibly. The words had to be gentle. She moved forward too, stopped at a certain point, and gazed at him. He held the bouquet out to her, came near, and kissed her eyelids, moving his fingers across her proffered face.

Bachir felt the woman's palpitating nostrils and the light pulse of her temples in his palms. He pressed his hands against the wall, as though embracing the glimpsed flesh.

The man slid the bolt into place and caught the woman as she threw herself into his arms. They melded together like eucalyptus branch and vine. A single tree rose in the middle of the room, tumultuous and burgeoning. Its extremities swayed in an exchange of embraces that made it lean nearer the bed at each moment until it finally collapsed. Bachir gripped the window firmly in order not to miss what was just beginning.

The woman was stretched out below the man; their hair mingled. A golden spray moved on the sheet, flamed up in the light and suddenly congealed. The mimosa blossoms slowly slid toward the wall, attracted by an invisible patch of shadow. The marabout stretched his hand over the moaning woman's belly. He recited grave and muddled words that no one understood. The name of Allah fell like a dry fruit onto the pale flanks buried in the thick wool rug. The woman was still lamenting. The marabout stood up, pulled a hair from his beard and pressed it into the amulet along with moistened herbs. He waved the silver case back and forth above her cries. The voice immediately abated, and calmer breathing rose from the soothed breast.

The man pressed the woman's temples in his palms. He caressed her face, stroked her neck, edged her ears. Bachir's moist lips were fixed on the Roumie's cheek. Torrid spittle moistened his tongue, and his heart beat in his throat.

She-goats were frisking down the cliff, dancing on their dainty hooves. Bachir caught one of them, muzzled it and held it in his arm. He felt it struggling against him, anxious and convulsive, and already savoured the moment when he would stretch out with it, fitting his body perfectly into a somber dip in the shadow of a cypress, a natural shell within which he could move easily, full of the odours, rebuffs and silences of the animal which would finally give up and doze with him below the earth's crust, in the hollow of the world, far from the roots that tear the skin and the stones that flay the feet, far from Allah, from screams, far from withered bellies, blood, cockroaches and the smell of mould, far from toilets and masters, far from Roumies' cars and their big glaucous eyes, very far, at the furthest point from everything that caused suffering.

The man's hands slipped snake-like over the woman's light skin. They brushed her shoulders, moving in circles over her back, her waist, and rose to her breast where they turned crazily, faster than the movement of the earth, to reach two buttercups that were melting in the sun. The rotation continued joyously about the axis the hands were dexterously moulding. Bachir observed this skillful work. He dug his fingers frantically into the lump of clay he had ripped out of the bank, convinced he would never have been able to operate so adroitly. Propelled by the need to appease his desire, he would have ground the flesh instead of caressing it and burst the fragile cone before he'd even rounded it out.

"You're crazy," clucked his cousin opening her legs a bit more. He rounded her ankle, and rose quickly to her hips without lingering at her thighs. He reached her loins and clung there, soon feeling a burgeoning swell against his fingers. In the shadow of the gandoura, a blossom was opening into his palm. He touched it softly at first, trying to feel the contours of the elusive petals, catching them, pressing them together and crumpling them savagely. The iris closed. His hand was swallowed by its bulbous stem, drawn into the narrow passage he explored and tore open. His cousin pushed him away. She readjusted her golden belt and got up in tears: "I'm not a virgin anymore. It'll be your fault if I don't find a husband."

He slipped away, fleeing the father who would have killed him had he known. For the moment he was sprawled among the cushions and skirts in the next room. Bachir need not worry. He would have the time to make the rounds of the douar before the father regained his senses. The half-light in the rooms had made him forget the sun's violence. His head burnt. Sweat ran down under his shirt. The cicadas and crickets sharpened their wings in fierce stridulation. Insects buzzed between his fingers, attracted by the scent of the blue iris.

He started running, crazed with rage and desire. He crashed down the hill, knocking violently into eucalyptus trees. Rolling on the ground, he could not extinguish the fire that devoured him. The earth repelled him. He beat himself furiously on the rough grass and found no freshness to bring relief. There was nothing left but to go back up to the rooms where his huddled cousins were dabbing at their foreheads and arms. He would return to those exhalations while there was still time. The celebrations would end tonight. At dawn they would leave the house, veiled, untouchable, and he would not be able to talk to them or even look at them anymore.

Through the window Bachir looked at the blonde woman's bare skin. Suddenly he rejected the falsely submissive women, the beribboned semi-virgins whose violence wore itself out behind closed shutters. Women whose patience would one day fade away leaving them with nothing more than a residue of illusions, a body left to its fits and silent rage. He liked tender gentle women, ageless like his mother, Malika, but there were few of them. They were hidden away like shameful objects, kept separate from men, from the open air and the light. They were shut away like wild beasts, dark panthers who would sometimes roar in their courtyards, frightening chickens, dogs and children, but would draw back their claws as soon as a male appeared.

Malika was unique. She sang while she kneaded the bread, spun the wool and rolled the couscous. Every morning she took him to pick olives. She was beautiful, still fresh and lively before the heat of the day. She would walk ahead, supple as a gazelle, her delicate hips swaying the crimson skirt that raised the dust around her bare feet. She would flag at noon and collapse on the mattress; each time he was afraid she would stay there. The child would hold his breath. Finally Malika would awaken. She would open her eyes and sit up, her long hair draped about her. She was his queen. He did not dare speak to her or approach her. Only when she went to the lean-to to get a handful of dried figs would he come near.

One day Malika lay down and did not get up again. They dressed her in white, smoothed her hair and covered her face with a mask. She stayed like that for twenty-four hours, surrounded by hired mourners who shook the walls with their lamentations. Men came, placed her on a canopied stretcher and carried her to the edge of the road where they laid her in a bed of sand. The earth was filled in and marked with whitewashed stones. The next day the bread and figs set next to her were gone. Malika had made the long journey to the Prophet. She had crossed the Rummel. She had risen higher than the birds, higher than the sun and the stars, to the place where a majestic seat, precious stones and embroided gandouras awaited her.

The man raised himself slightly on his elbows and kissed his wife's eyelids. Suffused with light, she rested on the bed, head tipped back, lips half-open. Bachir wondered if it was the sun or her happiness that made her so luminous. Her long hair mingled with the mimosa blossoms scattered on the sheet and formed a golden harvest that was more beautiful than the one in the valley of the douar in July.

Her eyes opened. She inclined her head and smiled. The man pressed her to him. While on his knees he ran his fingers over her lips, her throat, her belly and her open thighs. He drank in the joyful body he was softly touching. Again he covered the woman and lost himself in her. Together they turned in pools of fire, coiling about each other and tumbling in emptiness. Then they collapsed, their faces bathed in ecstasy. Flies approched. The woman woke from her dream and gazed at the man who wordlessly, even motionlessly, continued to love her.

Bachir could not bear the scene any longer. His cousins were laughing in the corners, capricious, immodest, drawing up inventories of jewels, ornaments and engagements for him which left him cold. He was sensitive to only one thing. Sex was everywhere, in the tone of their voices and the scent of their underarms. She-goats were frisking down the cliff, and dancing tongues of flame stirred his lower belly and lit up the lip of the well hung with empty buckets. Blue irises surged out from the silk cushions and flowered the tiles of the room. Moisture covered the walls with moss and fastened purplish stems to the closed shutters against which blind butterflies shattered. At the gateway to the desert, venomous snakes pounced in the prolific, disquieting vegetation.

It was the dry season. Lungs burst in the stifling heat. Bachir heard the orchestra roll out its Andalusian music in the main hall. The guitar gave the melody, hesitated, and held back the singer's cry as long as possible, finally bursting violently, almost brutally. The first wife was rich. She decorated the house with fine rugs, feather pillows and precious platters. She brought her husband herds of goats and sheep, houses and fields. Under her rule, the yard was full of pigeons, beehives and olive trees. And she served good black coffee and fine white couscous. But he had grown tired of her and taken another wife. His fortune was snuffed out immediately. He became poor and lost everyone's respect. "It's your fault, it's your fault," they all repeated in chorus.

Bachir paid no attention to the moral of the song. He only listened to the sound of the guitar and the violins, the heavy beat that stressed the rhythm and turned his heart around. All the pain, all the desire and the suffering of the world swelled the trailing voice that modulated the dream. Bachir's anger growled. He rolled on the ground moaning. There was no remedy for his pain. He would never have enough money to pay the dowry and embrace a woman who would be his own.

This evening, if he wanted, he had only to slip into a corner of the hall to watch them dance. He would see them strutting in his face and attend the display of white flesh and blonde hair without any hope of profiting from it. Tomorrow he would return to his brooms, toilets and goats. He would say: " Good day, sir. Yes, ma'am." He would drag his bare feet over the tiles and pick up one by one the mimosa blossoms left on the bed in number four.

A grasshopper brushed his throat. He crushed it in his fingers and hurled it against the wall.

4
The Cat

On Sunday afternoons the dining room of the Belvedere looked sad. The tables, set up in tight rows, seemed ready for the arrival of hordes of tourists. But there was not a single one.

The bay poured a white light over the parquet floor that flattened out shapes, congealing them in a dull non-reality. The crackling of the sun on the roof made the air heavy. Geneviève and Barbara stopped and surveyed the room suddenly struck by a shared impression.

"You'd never think we danced here last night."

"No, you'd never think that."

On one side, lay the sea; on the other, the patio edged with bougainvillea which led to the rooms. The play of shimmering shadows linked two contradictory worlds: the day with its prosaic realities and the night with its possible openings toward dreams and the needs of the heart. Overcome by a torpor which contrasted with the animation of that Saturday evening, Barbara discontinued her reflection. She began to talk, to ward off the silence. Geneviève responded in an acrid tone touched with fatigue.

At the far end of the room, two drowsy men were leaning on the bar. They too seemed to be in slow motion, engaged in desultory conversation. Barbara approached them, looked at the foam that topped their glasses and made a gesture of disgust.

" You're drinking that!"

" Yes, ma'am. Cheers!"

The taller of the two raised his glass and made a deep bow. The other one imitated the gesture hardly bending his shoulders. Geneviève commented on his lack of enthusiasm. He replied that not once in his life had he kneeled to anyone, but she did not seem to catch the allusion. He was insistent, repeating: " Me, that's who I am." She realised it was not his first drink.

" We ought to go."

" Go now? You're totally crazy."

" You won't be able to drive."

" All I need is one more drink to have perfect vision."

" Well, hurry up and finish."

" What's the rush? Waiter, would you get them a drink."

Aware that alcohol would be out of place, the waiter took two bottles of Fanta out of the fridge and served them to the women. For reasons of economy as much as of principle they refused alcohol whenever their men abused it. They accepted the lemonade graciously. Experience had taught them that an annoyed husband drinks twice as much. They turned toward the sea. The sun, though still high, was quickly going down. Half the beach already lay in shadows. The bathers moved away from the rocks and nearer to the water where no tree tempered the warmth of the day's end.

"It's depressing," Barbara remarked.

Shouts rose from the base of the cliff, muffled by the distance and mingled with the hum that spread along the shore. A group of children ran to take a last swim. Goats left the grass and came down to stretch out under the eucalyptus trees. Something irremediable was happening. The weekend holiday was drawing to a close.

"I could sleep for an hour."

"We have to be getting back."

"You only have one life and you can't even sleep it in peace."

"Oh, don't make phrases. Coming from you they sound hollow."

"Come now, children, finish your drinks without arguing. We have a two-hour drive ahead of us."

Geneviève disliked sharp exchanges between what she called "a couple." The men remained deaf to her advice, commenting that they always started back too early, that visibility was nil when the sun hit the windshield horizontally, and this caused undue risks. In this argument the women recognised the prelude to another beer. They looked at each other in despair.

"Did you pay for the rooms?"

"Not yet."

The waiter respectfully brought the bill and pointed at the bottom line.

"I left it blank for the beer."

"Left it blank for the beer! How thoughtful. And only one bill as usual."

"You are brothers, no?"

Since the hotel personnel had decided they were brothers, it was no use arguing the point. The colour of the skin, the eyes, and beards carried more weight than any discussion. As for the hair, it was well known that Roumies had the habit of splitting hairs. They always got tangled up in useless convolutions explaining that they were not of the same stock and did not even come from the same place. They belonged to neither clan nor town. They were born alone and would die alone, as they had done for centuries.

"Cheers, brother."

Barbara sighed. She knew how this would go on. An hour would pass, and they would still be at the bar mulling over their gripes. They would spout their usual reflections on the native population, wear themselves out with endless recriminations and return to town, dazed and depressed. Powerless against the real culprits, she made the room responsible.

"Sundays there's not even a cat in this tomb!"

She had hardly uttered the sentence when a small plump man appeared in the doorway. He had a round head, feline eyes and a moustache pulled toward his cheeks. He said: "Hello!" — and headed straight toward them. Then he smiled and held out the claws of his short chubby hand to each one.

"Good thing you're here! Last time I came it was completely dead!"

His sudden presence created a welcome diversion. The man licked his lips, looking for pleasant things to add. He spoke with a strong foreign accent.

"Are you American?"

"No, but I've lived in America. I've been around just about everywhere, you know."

"You have an English accent."

"Oh accents, I must have five or six of them. I can say *I love you* in every language. Even Japanese."

"Go ahead."

"I'm afraid I'll make the ladies blush. Actually, should I be saying *ladies* or *girls*?"

"That's for you to decide."

"I wouldn't decide. I'm stating a fact. You have the freshness of young girls, but you're wearing wedding bands. Take them off, and I'll call you *miss*."

They were no longer alone. A newcomer was speaking. They were gripped by a certain frenzy, as though the half-light stagnating at the windows no longer threatened them. Time was perceptible again. Someone was momentarily delivering them from tedium.

"Say, what's that you're drinking? Beer? Cognac is what you need at this time of day. Waiter, five double cognacs."

He led them to a table set in the window overlooking the terrace, then sat down first and invited the men to take a seat, while he kept the women at his sides.

"I like to be surrounded by pretty women. Life is short, you have to make the most of it."

"Are you working here?"

"Working? Not exactly. Actually, I make others work."

"In what field?"

"I'm an engineer. A project involving three hundred men. And as far as work is concerned, I can promise you they work. As soon as they start to slacken off, I shout *Hemchi* and send them packing to their fathers."

"Is it easy to find other workers?"

"They're not workers, they're trainees. When they arrive, they hardly know the difference between a straight line and a curve. Last week I had the same string laid three times, and it was still off. 'Okay,' I said, 'that's it for you, wog.'"

"You're a hard man."

"That's how I am with men. With women I'm sweetness personified."

He stretched one paw toward Barbara. She laughed, stiffening a little. The waiter put the cognacs on the table. Yellow flowers that stained the tablecloth. The afternoon wore on comfortably thanks to this man who spoke six languages and let them forget time.

"Cheers! It's been a long time since I had a drink in such pleasant company. And God knows, I've made toasts in my life. I've clinked glasses in the world's best cabarets. Paris, London, Istanbul, Tokyo, Baghdad. Do you know the belly dance?"

"It's not very good here, and you know, we haven't been around the world."

"Oh, you ought to. Take me, I'm like God, I want to see everything."

"Another one who thinks he's the Prophet. How many women have you had?"

"I haven't enough fingers to count them on. I've had them in all colours, but I have a weakness for Japanese women. Nothing can beat them. At Osaka, I kept one with me for a week. When I left, she cried like a baby."

"You must be quite irresistible."

"It's a question of style. You have it, or you don't. And you two... I bet you don't have it."

Both men leapt up and hit the table with their softened fists. The shorter one quickly sat down again. The other one remained standing ready to strangle this brute that had dared to insult him.

"That's an insult! You don't know who you're talking to. You forget that I have Viking blood in my veins."

"Viking blood? I have some too. My maternal grandfather was from Brittany. That's served me well in my life. Thank God, I had Breton blood in my veins at Shiprock."

"What were you doing down there?"

"Smuggling gold. In two weeks I made half a million."

"Don't you have a litle left? We could split it."

"No. I lost everything in Reno in three days. Not a penny left. I told myself it's not the end of the world, I'll have to start again at zero. I found someone to pay my ticket and left for Rhodesia."

"Where you put a quite insignificant little diamond into your pocket."

"Yes, a diamond, and that was worse than if I'd found gold. A prospector accused me of having stolen it and told me to clear out. Two hours later I served him a special drink and he left first."

"You're a real fiend."

"A fiend? No. I'm a pussycat. I can squeeze into spots where others can't even get a little finger."

Barbara looked at the man. He did look like a cat and had a cat's reactions, its face, its suppleness. His chubby hands softly stroked the glass and rose to cross below his throat which emitted a rough whistle between sentences. In the dark, his eyes were probably green. The sun was no more than a thin fiery band above the sea. She shivered, despite the heat, thinking he could well become dangerous once night fell. Screaming would have made her feel better.

"We should be going if we don't want to be on the road in the dark."

"Go? But we're getting to know each other."

"Don't provoke her. She'll start roaring like a panther."

"A blonde panther. I've never seen one of them. And never with such lovely eyes. I'd say she is more like the young guanacos on Tierra del Fuego. A gentle disposition, charm, kindness, but if you approach them too roughly, they bite your hand or spit in your face."

"Me, that's who I am. And if you're rude to my wife, I'll make you pay for it."

"How much are you asking?"

"Take that back! Right now!"

The angry husband hit the table with a soft fist that did not frighten anyone. Appearing not to see or hear anything, the stranger opened his wallet and took out a wad of hundred dinar bills that he spread on the tablecloth. He riffled the money skillfully yet indifferently as though it were a pack of cards. But the greed in his eyes belied this attitude.

"This is the source of power! There are two categories of people in the world: men and wogs. And men cannot do without this."

"Or this," Barbara said, indicating her head.

"Intelligence only makes your capital yield a profit. Am I shocking you? You're young, and you haven't travelled. This is where the future of the world is and nowhere else. If you don't own anything, you are sub-human."

He spoke to her patronisingly. Barbara felt herself touch a critical limit she was afraid of crossing, as though getting bogged down in indolence preserved her from the fear of taking a stand. They had all failed in this city with their prejudices and their habits. Reading Kierkegaard's *Treatise on Despair* or the Epistle on forgiveness by Abou El Alaal Maari led to the same commonplace: women were either mothers or whores. The servants, whose services they exploited for the moment, freed them from domestic labour without changing their status or their function.

Geneviève, content to listen up till then, lit a cigarette and tore the air with a burst of laughter. The stranger took this as encouragement and stroked her thigh while his hand held Barbara's wrist.

"I am a romantic, you know. See that sunset? That's nothing next to all the ones I've seen in my life. From country to country they are never the same colour. In China they were purple. In Mexico they tended more to apricot and orange. In the Congo, violet was the main colour. Turkey, that was the ultimate. At Edirne, the sun drops into the Maritsa like a fiery ball swallowed by a green eye."

"Green?"

"Green, lots of green. The most beautiful sunsets are green. It was a rare green. Something like the colour of your eyes."

"They've never been green."

"When you look at the Mediterranean, they turn green. It's too bad you have to get back. I would have taken you out for a little cruise, all four of you. I like to make people happy."

He babbled on about the beaches he had visited, the faces he had nibbled at on moist nights in the depths of rooms without locks or bedsheets, or on the sands of deserted shores where the charm that had led him there soon vanished far away. It was a small world and he revolved about it like an automaton, loaded with old memories that he regilded, reassured by the constancy of a face and someone's permanent loyalty.

"Everytime I travel, I send my wife a postcard. She has a huge collection of them. Look, here's a photo of her."

He took the wallet he had left on the table and extracted a tiny photograph from it. A young dark-haired woman regarded them sadly, with the look of someone disappointed in love who had learnt about it only in novels. She had a low forehead, a drooping mouth, and the look of a frightened doe put her undeniably into the wog category. A moment of embarassment hung over the group. The cat put away the photo.

"Does it surprise you that I have such a young wife?"

"Oh, the age difference is not important."

"Difference! That's the question. Take these two beauties here: if they underwent a sex change, we'd never get over it."

One of the husbands raised his voice, happy to put in a word.

"I repeat they are not for sale, and me, that's who I am."

65

"And that's what breaks my heart. I'd like to see the four of you again. Do you come here to dance now and then?"

"Dance? That's all they do! Our wives discovered their vocation in North Africa. They were born to dance."

"Is that so? We'll see each other again then? When will you be back?"

"Thursday."

The men gave a start.

"Because now, besides going dancing on Saturdays, we're going on Thursdays too?"

"From now on, we're not coming on Saturdays anymore, just on Thursdays. That way we'll get home earlier."

Under this threat, the men got up. They said their goodbyes to the cat with somewhat sagging knees. The women shook his hand and fled, repeating: "See you Thursday!"

He replied: "I'll be there" — quivering with pleasure. The sea had turned grey. Silence enveloped the coast and reached the Belvedere. Within the hour the road would be in darkness.

Barbara whispered into Geneviève's ear: "Are we really coming here to dance on Thursday?"

"No, that was a trap."

"What a revolting man! I feel like puking and we haven't even gotten to the bends yet."

She brought her hand to her mouth and suppressed a hiccup. Geneviève burst out laughing and admitted the cognac had made

66

her feel better. At the door they looked back. He was standing beside the table making them a sign with his hand. Against the matte background of the window, he had the shape of an alley cat.

Henna for Luck

In the middle of the dance floor, Slimane danced alone.

His head pressed into empty space, he held himself upright, one leg supporting his slender body below the darkness of the ceiling. The moment of support between steps was so short that the two leaps melted into the single throb of a meticulous chassé. It was executed beyond thought and space, only by the thrust of instinct, or of delirium. This was the impression of some of the onlookers watching the big black bird locked in a ferocious battle with the ground, its delicate frame ceaselessly wrenching itself away, trying to free itself, keeping them all cowering in anxiety — the two Vikings, the Saint-Bernard, Geneviève, Barbara and the others, all those who knew the story and were expecting the worst.

Slimane was relieved of the waiting and the fear. He continued dancing, effortlessly keeping time with the charleston now risen to fever pitch, threatening to suffocate the audience which was unable to endure the frenzied passion any longer, the convulsive fury that recalled the spell-binding trances of firebreathers. They were all observing him with a consternation combined with fear and pity. The scene would continue to unfold, or end, leaving them with a skeleton they would not know what to do with: a livid body with a haggard, crazed head, detached from the music and rolling at their feet, that would return to haunt them at night.

They could not forget Slimane's silhouette leaping from rock to rock, his dark eyes suddenly becoming glassy, his animal cry echoed by the mountain, his silence, and finally his unrestrained grief. They recalled seeing his body lying next to the young girl's, their heads tipped back in the murderous sunlight, their legs bent and lapped by the indifferent waves. All around nothing had changed. There was the foam splattering the cliff, the crowd of bathers running and shouting amid the parasols stuck into the burning sand, the rounds of the watermelon sellers, the absurd silence of the sky, the fishing boats moored as before, as always, since the beginning of summer.

Into this shimmering light and distant hum: Slimane's sudden awakening. They could not wipe away the memory of the boy's arms circling the girl, urging her to get up, his perseverance, his relentless repetition of a name to which she remained deaf. *Fadila! Fadila!* She no longer saw the sky, or the sea, or anyone. She did not feel the hands that caressed her, touching her ears, her mouth, her cheeks, and suddenly freezing at the left temple.

Slimane's fingers were stained with an accursed blood that no salvo of shots would acclaim in the rituals of defloration. The bridegroom would not be led in triumph from the nuptial chamber to join the men. The women would not cry behind the partitions and would not give way to excessive rejoicing. They would not snatch for the nightdress to check the signs, still warm, of conquered virginity. They would search in vain under Fadila's pillow for the tiny knife and the mirror set in silver.

Beauty and audacity had escaped the rites of the tribe. They lay at the foot of the cliff, accusing, forming an unbearable stain of light. The onlookers shivered in spite of the heat. They moved away softly, overwhelmed by the inevitable that no derisive comment could reduce to chance.

"It's incredible!" said the Saint-Bernard.

Geneviève shared this opinion and added: " It's absurd."

Slimane heard nothing.

He was dancing, sweat streaming down his forehead. The men had begun to clap their hands. Their applause stressed the rhythm, splintering it into motifs that rebounded between the boy's legs forcing him to move even faster. Fadila's steps took shape between his. They crunched the gravel along the edge of the road, shook the noontime torpor, drowned out the lapping of the waves and the droning of cars.

One of the cars stopped, ready to seize the prey slipping away into the light. The young woman plunged down the bank and disappeared into the brush, fleeing the cliff road and the ambushes awaiting her there.

"Where are you going?"

"You want to come for a ride?"

"Get in, or I'll take you home to your father!"

She took a path already trodden by goats, readjusted her headscarf and did up the overcoat that covered her white arms, her pink gandoura, her golden jewelry. Her charms were well protected. She would be able to defend them against any violation.

She was almost running, resolved to take the fate she had been denied into her own hands. She would hold it for only a second, and no one would be able to stop her, not even the man taking part in the offensive festivities. The cicadas' song had become too shrill. This strident summer noise was as exhausting as running in the sun. Fadila slumped under a tree and examined the area to make sure she was alone.

Reassured, she leaned her head against the tree and closed her eyes. Rid of onlookers, she felt the life pulsing within her more clearly. This flight contrasted with habits of languour and ease. She heard the sea nearby, its cradling rhythm. And words came back to her, inexhaustible, like her pain.

"Fadila, you're the most beautiful girl I know."

"Say it again."

"You're the most beautiful woman of all."

Two ardent eyes were resting on her. Pressed to Slimane, she matched his passion, and dreaded his demands and fits of rage.

" Will you always love me?"

" I'll love you as long as there are stars."

" Here, you don't marry who you want."

He shushed her.

They had been able to choose, others would do the same. She let herself be convinced, more sensitive to reasons of the flesh than to the force of the argument. This love, that sometimes took the form of combat, brought her the feeling of a definitive power, the knowledge of a superior state for which others envied them. She loved the gentleness of their relations, but also the violent confrontations that pitted them one against the other until their lips drew close in the same uneasy surge.

Exhausted, Fadila brushed at the mosquitoes on her face while Slimane continued dancing. As soon as she felt the thrust shake the boy's body, she got up, put on her coat and covered her hair. He leapt up, amassing shadow around his shoulders while she rushed out into the blinding light , propelled by a rhythm as demanding as the orchestra's. Her hands lifted her skirt off the tufts of broom and smoothed it down over her knees in two silky panels that swished under the stiff fabric of the coat.

She was running, skirting the narrow bays between the rocks and climbing up the cliff grasping onto the roots of the scorched cedars.

She avoided looking at the light sand of the shore, the clusters of mimosa in bloom, the slow swell that licked the beach. She distrusted the gentleness of the landscape. To strengthen her resolve she revived the anger that had possessed her for two weeks. Two weeks of fury during which she had at first collapsed in despair, wallowed in laments, then had straightened up, resolved and complete. It was six o'clock in the evening. A sudden determination had come over her; at first she had considered it coldly, then accepted it as irremediable.

The bay was dipping its bright belly into the sea. She looked out beyond the last rock into the cove where the waves were breaking on the stones. Fadila recalled the broken rock at this spot, its points biting into the sky, the unyielding violence of its spurs and crests. She found its rugged shape again, located the narrow gorge between the escarpments into which she had followed Slimane who was pulling her forward crying: "Don't leave me!" They were trampling down a patch of red grass. She was clinging to him, torn between two attractions. The immense, roaring sea behind her, beating the invisible earth. He, in front, laughing, his face almost white. She understood his desire to open her savagely on this patch of grass, and his wish, equally strong, to keep her intact for the approaching wedding night.

Somber, almost tragic, the bridegroom was distractedly receiving good wishes.

"May you have a long life, Slimane!"

"We wish you a boy as your first-born!"

"May the blessings of Allah accompany you to the end of your days!"

Allah and the lineage were a single branch, an indestructible tree to which Slimane had become attached. The country was swarming with children, yet women wanted more. The midwives were never done cutting the umbilical cords of the newborn, and the circumcision rituals mingled their scraps of dead flesh with the putrified bodies piled in the ancestral gardens. The chainlinking of the sexes created a kingdom of males, but life relentlessly devoured what the women's bodies strained to produce.

Before he went to fetch his bride from her home, a baby had been laid into her arms to ensure her fertility. The old women whispering in the corners assessed the bride's chances and found her hips narrow, her chest hollow. Oh Fadila, so beautiful and complete in her shapely curves! Fadila, so happy in her body and soul! Fadila, languishing in the sun and revived at night by the scent of jasmine, where was she? Why was she not a part of these brilliant ceremonies?

She was approaching, touching the rock whose dry grain she recognised, its spurs jutting sharply into empty space. She stepped back, examined the islet of red grass, and then stretched out alone in the shadowy groove that fitted her body perfectly. Music exploded in her head and made a long shiver run down her body. She stood up, came back into the sunlight, took off her coat, her shoes, her golden belt. The gandoura billowed out. Breathless, Fadila undid the scarf that held her hair and tilting her head made the shimmering mass fall over her forehead. She moved to the outermost point of the rock, seeing nothing but hair and the foamy crests of the breakers far below.

A cry escaped from the bridegroom's throat and he refused to dance any longer. But they forced him to continue, dragging him out in front of the orchestra. For the benefit of the males, he was to roll his hips and display his body, perform the gesture of solitary pleasure and prolong the ritual intoxication. The tribe required this spectacle and demanded these pleasures as a distraction from the gloom of daily life. "Dance, Slimane!" And the orchestra scraped its strings and beat its drums drawing out the harsh and nasal sabre dance below the ballroom ceiling. Slimane, a false Tuareg, slashed the space with large blows, his left foot slipping on the tiles, his right bracing itself against the thrust of the knife.

His mother drew back, livid.

"Slimane, you don't have the right!"

He moved forward threateningly, his arms reducing the distance between him and the woman. "You'll be damned!" Before the hell opening up, the prohibitions, and the power of the clan, he was yielding and consenting to

75

incest. He gave way before the woman who was taking Fadila away from him and imposing her niece, a thin girl he had seen only occasionally at funerals. Thus the blood-line would not suffer division. It would return to the tribe as the Rummel had been flowing into the sea for centuries.

The celebration was continuing, carried along by the music that beat out the rhythm of the festivities. People gorged themselves on kebabs, couscous, honey cakes and almonds. The women bustled about showing off their clothes and jewels. In a separate group, the men regaled themselves with rampant lechery. The rejoicing would continue for seven days. Then the clamp would snap down on the couple, and Slimane would be bored for the rest of his life. This evening he would join the bride, and in the shadows of the bedroom, his arms would welcome a stranger who would reawaken his hatred for his mother.

His heart stayed cold, attached to Fadila who was running and knocking on neighbours' doors.

"If I've ever offended you, please forgive me."

Frightened,the women immediately closed their doors. They hid behind the shutters and watched the child who was doomed by the Prophet's curse.

Fadila went back up the street, crossed the square without looking back, skirted Sidi Benmalek's newspaper stand, and climbed the steps that led to the baths. She entered, paying the matron, and crossing through the empty and silent main bath, she went to the room reserved for brides. In the alcove she undid her hair, took off her dress and wearily looked at her body. It was virgin, as intact as the day she was born. No one had really touched it, not even Slimane who had promised to marry it.

Wrapping herself in a towel, she approached the water and sank slowly into it. Air bubbles formed around her. She burst them one by one surrounding herself with total emptiness before she lathered her body with soap. The water slipped between her breasts and ran down her flat belly, waking a great sadness in her. She twisted her hair, and lay on her back floating in the foam forcing herself to think of nothing. New bubbles appeared; she burst them in a state of dizzy exhaustion. Time congealed. She managed to forget who she was and why she had come to the baths.

The matron was getting impatient. Fadila had to get out of the water and dry off. They gave her oil and powder and perfume. They rubbed her feet and hands with "Henna for Blissful Nights," as the label on the bottle promised. She put on the velvet gandoura, bedecked herself with her jewels, and did her hair. She brushed her eyebrows and edged her eyes with khol. An empty face gazed back from the mirror they held for her.

She cast a quick glance at this forbidden beauty she was no longer consciously inhabiting and got up. She had to leave the reassuring shade of the baths, forget the steaming heat that had soothed her. She had to go out to confront the sun and exorcise her fear. The old woman's admiring glance followed her, confirming her status as a desirable creature. She lowered her eyes.

Abruptly the bridegroom reared up and tore himself out of the rhythm that was making his body sway continuously. He regained his balance, reducing the spasms that continued to shake his hips after his torso had already stopped moving. Men surrounded him. He broke through the group and rushed to the exit.

Outside, the heat was torrid. He turned his back to the sun and looked at the sea. This liquid opening made him shiver. He leaned against the freshly whitewashed garden gates and vomited. Then he raised his head. Without turning back, he went through the gateway scented with mint, determined to get away.

A cry rose from the far point of the cliff. He began to run in the direction of the cry. His instinct told him which shortcuts to take, which crevasses to avoid. It led him straight to his goal, the far point of the headland where the coast closes on an eddy pulled in by the breakers.

Below, the light fell on a rock spattered with blood. A second, final cry rose. The man fell to the ground, collapsed in pain. He lay moaning before the people fascinated by the horror.

"Did it last a long time?"

"A good half hour."

"Have the mourners come?"

"No. Tomorrow they'll go to the girl's parents."

"Have the police been notified?"

"Probably, we didn't stay till the end."

"It's unbelievable."

Geneviève was repeating it a second time. Barbara took no notice; neither did the two Vikings and the big Saint-Bernard. Seated at their usual table, they sipped their whisky bewitched by the dancer.

No one else was on the dance floor. All alone, Slimane was grinding up the space, his face an expression of unbearable fury. Convulsions rattled his torso, delivering up his body to frenzied distortion. The pain was violent, spellbinding.

"Do you think he's lost his mind?"

"Very likely."

Welcome

The man downed his coffee in one gulp and pushed the tray to the edge of the table. The heat was unbearable on the hotel terrace. He had hoped for a bit of fresh air from the sea, but gazing at the shimmering expanse where a few swimmers were already bobbing, he saw that it would be another oppressive day.

Would she like this new country? He remembered the smells, the impressions he had imbibed on his first day, and never forgotten. This prompted him to design an inviting welcome, a quick trip through the city along the more elegant streets and then, right away, the asphalt road along the coast. The light would flood the car windshield. Amazed, she would bathe in the phosphorescent summer streaming over her face.

She would notice the clumps of mimosa that concealed the hotel, the splash of the geraniums as soon as they rounded the corner, the play of shadow and light below the patio arches. She would ask to go down to the beach, dig her bare feet into the burning sand and throw herself tumbling into the sea. He would follow, and reach her in the flashes in which she submerged, open to the ground swells of the fabled desert whose rites and mirages she would share with him.

Their old madness would resurge. He would take her to Sidi Benmalek's bamboo kiosk, and order a well-chilled rosé and fresh mullets. Then they would return to the hotel along a shady path, and he would bedeck her with orange blossoms like a bride. Instinctively their bodies would rediscover the network of old complicities and wonder. Once in the room, they would close the blinds and pursue their fascination to the end, fall onto the shaky bed and succumb to the frenzy of love.

Only then would he dare take her back to the city and have her climb the five flights of stairs of the city housing block where he had managed to find an apartment. He would precede her up the staircase, trying to conceal the garbage littering the ground floor and the obscene graffiti on the walls. He would bring her into the dining room sprayed with Vitox. She would see a few pieces of furniture, a bouquet of flowers on the table, flies stuck to the windowpanes that separated them from the blue evening beginning to fall, and she would approach the window to open the shutters.

The car went from the hotel to the airport, and he hardly felt the sudden braking in the curves, the bites of the yellow line, the many downshifts into second and changes back into third. He wondered if he had asked the *maître d'hôtel* to have the room cleaned before he got back. He did not remember leaving him the key. He hardly remembered getting up or shaving. In the arrival lounge he carefully put his bouquet of red roses on the table and ordered an aperitif.

The waiter dragged his slow steps across the tiles, and today this indolence annoyed him more than ever. To relieve his tension he gazed at the shadowy hole where the waiter had disappeared, and tried to empty his mind. A friend whose steps he did not hear, joined him and offered him a cigarette. Sun splattered the tablecloth with a blinding light. Heat crackled off the chairs on which they were sitting. He threw away his cigarette butt and crushed it under his heel.

" What time is it?"

" Nine-thirty."

" Your watch isn't slow?"

" It's fast if anything. I set it by the Tower of London."

Any other day he would probably have laughed at the joke. Today he found it clumsy. He began pacing on the terrace as though to accelerate the passage of time. The hands hardly moved over the face of his watch. He got tired of walking such a tight circle and sat down again. Two frosted glasses were put in front of them.

" Will that be all, sir?"

The waiter turned away, without waiting for an answer. He must have thought it crazy to expect anything from a foreigner. The friend caught him and tossed a handful of dinars onto the copper plate, then tried to attract the attention of his oblivious companion.

The mountains, grouped around the airport like a herd of dromedaries, stretched out in tight rows that gradually broke up until they were lost in the vague expanse where the desert began. The man would have liked to absorb the peace of the Sahara he could sense close behind the chain of the Aurès, where towns grew scarce, the air was pure, and the soil soon produced nothing but agaves and petrified time poured in stone which shattered duration. Gazing into this blank space, he imagined the dark line which would split the emptiness, separate heaven and earth, and approach the landing strip with two wings outstretched like wide-open arms.

Arid, dry faces stared at him. He felt the fine grain of the white skin on his chin and the difference between them. Behind him, people were leaving their chairs to cluster around the gangway. He pushed his way through the crowd of people clinging to the hot ramp, determined to defend their positions. Below, the rolling stairs were moving into place. A tank truck drove up, followed by mechanics in blue overalls. The wait could not last much longer.

" Five more minutes and I'll go crazy."

He did not hear his friend say he was dramatising a perfectly normal situation. He felt a sudden rush of blood to his temples and the tightening of an artery in the hollow of his diaphragm. A metallic crashing rattled his skull. He existed only in this noise that immobilised him. He closed his eyes and gripped his chest with both hands.

"Heh, don't let yourself go, good God! The Caravelle's here."

Regaining a grip on himself he risked a glance. The twin-engine plane was in fact on the strip. Hostesses were beginning to disembark, white scarves flapping like wings below their throats. They preceded the passengers and led them to the customs office. The man watched the procession closely. Then his voice broke.

"She's not there."

"She may still come."

"Impossible. Everyone's gotten off."

He stared at the wilting bouquet, the empty runway and waited, his eyes fixed on the open door of the motionless Caravelle. A spot of colour suddenly detached itself from the shadow at which he was staring, extended by a second one, as light and unclear. They grew deeper. They took on shape, shocking white and pink in this veiled land where flesh was proscribed. He recognised them. They were the only ones who could move so lightly, so easily, their feet hardly touching the ground. The only ones who could shake up this man's heart and wrench out the cries he could hardly contain.

His wife and daughter — and the tenacious spell he had never shaken — he wanted them clinging to his neck: their warm bodies pressed against his. He watched them come, laden with bags, suitcases, newspapers and understood why they were the last to get off. As usual, they had had to gather up from under their seats, all the useless things they were now dragging along with some difficulty. This mania for keeping everything close by had often exasperated him. Now he felt indulgent. He forgave them everything because they were coming to him, beautiful, essential, and a little crazy.

They were only a few metres from the airport building. Putting down their luggage, they answered his kisses. Their arms waved through the air excessively. They called out things better kept quiet. The girl showed him a long American Barbie fastened to her schoolbag. The woman tossed him a life-size Negro doll, with crisped hair, naked beneath her flowered dress. He received this gift, tucked it next to the bouquet of roses, and pressed it to him.

They disappeared into the customs office. He ran down the stairs that led to the arrivals lounge where his friend helped him push his way through the tangle of arms and legs in front of him. He finally reached the barrier and clutched on to it, trying to distinguish them in the crowd clustered at the counters. He finally glimpsed them at the end of the hall. The girl was rolling her coat up under her arm. The woman was writing, head bent forward, hair separated in two streams on each side of her neck. He would have given anything to touch the nape of that neck, but he knew he had not finished waiting.

She had always made him fill out the papers, claiming not to understand them. She was probably agonising over her statement of valuables right now. He watched her counting her rings and bracelets — she never knew exactly how many she had — and he would have liked to tell her to put an approximate figure, it did not matter anyway. Only one thing was important. To have her with him as quickly as possible.

He did not get the chance to give her this advice. A security guard touched him on the shoulder and asked him to come along. Two lines of police made a path through the crowd on either side of them. He walked along eagerly. He smiled appreciatively at this solemn way of emphasizing his family's arrival, and thought he saw a similar joy in the bystanders' faces. The guard stood aside at an open door. He entered. Officers were standing at attention. He resisted kissing one of them.

A customs officer stepped past the line and shouted: " The doll!" Grabbing it, he laid it on the table and took a knife from his pocket. The man dreaded what was about to happen. He saw the hand approach the bare belly. He heard the ripping noise, closed his eyes and suffered as he had on the day of his daughter's birth, when his wife's cries pierced the walls and made him scream too.

A metal object was laid on the table. The operation was over. The fabric was pulled back over the opened thighs before they returned the doll to him. He accepted it gingerly.

" We beg your pardon, sir."

He did not see their embarrassed gestures. He went out, taking the opposite direction down the passage left free by the silent crowd that now closed behind him.

Trivia

My country is a legend of rock and ice that chills you to the bone. The sun splinters into hard sparks there.

Zaina picks up the ice cubes one by one and licks them greedily. She never has any pocket money left to buy herself ice cream. She is saving up for the seven wedding gandouras, each a different colour, to celebrate the first seven days after the ceremony. She cannot explain why they are white or green or black or pink. Tradition cannot be explained. Nobody knows. She stops moving.

" The postman came twice today."

" Really?"

" Honestly! It's from over there."

Over there, is my country. Zaina sees it completely white, stretched out like a dune between tawny windswept trees. That is all she can imagine. The rest is lost in a vague expanse located on the other side of an immense body of water it takes six hours to cross by plane.

" There aren't any orange trees?

" No."

" What do you use to flavour cakes with?"

She asks me that for the hundredth time. I do not bother to answer anymore. Zaina likes hearing about my country. She listens, crouched on the floor, knees bent below her chin and her feet firmly on the tiles. "Over there," she says, "there are no dromedaries or scorpions or vines or palm trees." She works by process of elimination, with trees, animals and plants she knows, and when there is nothing left but the snow-covered ground she shivers and stops asking questions. That is when she comes out with the inevitable line: "See, it's a lot better here. We have sun and jasmine."

Zaina brings a big pair of scissors. When I have finished reading the letter she will cut out the picture of the Queen of England. All the girls in the building already have one in their wallets. They will wear a tiara like hers on their wedding day. Every week I get five or six stamps with her image, and Zaina is shocked to see me throw them in the wastebasket. She rescues them along with the runny tights and bits of thread that collect there. Nothing goes to waste with her. She would willingly trade my bra for a camel, if she had the chance.

"Did you live with her?"

"No."

"Did you know her well?"

"Quite well."

Zaina has read over my shoulder. Within the hour the whole building will know that Aunt Régine passed away, and by this evening the whole town will have heard. This is the most common type of telephone here. The smallest kitchen or bedroom secret spreads with dazzling speed. In no time, a tragedy is thickened and ripened by spittle and drops from the lips like a tasty morsel.

Trivia are the opium of the poor. You have to survive whichever way possible. The prices of butter and vegetables are exorbitant. If Zaina were queen, she would distribute free oil once a week. Queens are different from other women. They can do whatever they want. They wear rich jewels and are never beaten by their men. Zaina would love to be one.

Today, in late January, it is sixty degrees in the shade. An immense sun warms my shoulders. The window is so large that the two banks of the Rummel — the narrow thread of muddy water they call a river — are practically right in the living room, a noisy place that functions as library, dining room, family room, bedroom and even kitchen on the days when there is no electricity.

I hear the tenant from the fifth floor come down, as he does every day at this time. Children jostle each other on the ground floor and the city hums in the dust. Someone rings the doorbell. A ragged boy offers me Japanese porcelain cups. Zaina translates. He asks for old clothes and wishes me paradise when he gets some. People promise me paradise three or four times a week. The misery of others will end up being my salvation. Zaina watches me drink my Kebir rosé with a reproving glance. I will have to wash the glass myself; she refuses to touch it. The Iman has threatened her brother with hell for secretly drinking wine.

"I'd like to die," Zaina says. "You don't do a thing in Paradise. You sit and smell the trees and the fruit and the flowers. Everyone is equal. There aren't any ugly or handsome people like here. Everyone has the same face. First you are all dust. Then you grow a little, like mushrooms, head down, and stretch out until you become man or woman."

It is simple. You just have to think about it. If you avoid philosophising about death, it is a normal occurrence. "When the sun shines," Zaina says, "you smell the grass and the flowers. When it rains, you watch the rain fall to make the wheat grow and give the animals water. Then you eat the wheat, and once you've grown old you die and return to the earth."

She falls silent, overcome by her gloomy thoughts. For her, life is attached to two clumps of earth. But there are vistas of the beyond that make it grave and mysterious.

"It's sad, death."

"You think so?"

"If you're poor you can't go to Mecca, and then Paradise is lost."

She says: "I'll never be able to go there. Last year grandfather went to Mecca in his white gandoura and shoes and his white suit. In the mornings he would walk on the mountain and pray to God for everybody. He'd bow down and beg forgiveness for his sins, making sure to get up again quickly so the devil wouldn't draw him down to Hell. When he came home, you wouldn't see his face. He came in and knelt down in silence for hours. On the next day we slaughtered the sheep, and he gave us the gifts he had brought back, gold bracelets, earrings with pictures of Mecca, and green water to cure disease and prevent death."

The water of the Rummel is almost black. There is not enough rain. The earth is cracked everywhere. The banks that support the narrow bridge connecting us to the city are deeply fissured. If the fragile road surface ever succumbs despite the work crews' constant repairs, we will be completely isolated, unable to support ourselves. In this torrid climate, there are great extremes. On rainy days the mud clogs up the streets, the entrance, the ground floor. Then Zaina uses large buckets of water to flush it out to where the wind finally dries it.

I lounge in front of the open window, softly reclining in the garden chair brought from over there. There is no garden or balcony here, but it is still convenient to have the chair. It is more comfortable than the couch made from packing cases. Wrapped in oblivion and warmth, I no longer feel my body. It purrs like a cat, hardly distracted by the stories it hears.

"The good people go to Paradise," Zaina continues, "and the bad ones go to Hell. When they arrive, the Prophet is in a big armchair and he raises his arm, once to the right to let the good ones into Paradise, twice to the left to send the bad ones to Hell."

Her large gesture splits the air in two. She would not mind dealing out justice. I would find it rather difficult. I would not know on which side to weight the scales. I would probably send everybody to Paradise to avoid the trouble of sorting out their guilty consciences or family squabbles. I would not feel very proud either, having to demand explanations. After all they never asked to live or die. It happened to them regardless.

I wonder how old Aunt Régine was. Certainly more than sixty. Sixty is twice my age, and it is still not very old when I look at how far I have gotten. What I have accomplished anyone else could have done in my stead. Everyone, just about, can produce children and earn their living. At twenty, you dream of unparalleled adventures, but everyone ends up at the same place.

"The Prophet doesn't care if you're sick. The marabouts are in charge of those things. You go see them if you want to get better, pass an exam, or find a husband. You tell them: 'If you cure my sister, I'll buy a big rug.' He gives you something to burn or smell, and things happen. My cousin didn't have any children for ten years. After she went to the marabout, she had a boy. They bought a sheep, invited all the neighbours and had a big feast to celebrate the miracle. The couscous lasted seven days."

A smile lights up the child-woman's face as she twists the gold bracelets on her arm.

" Are there marabouts in your country?"

" No."

" If she'd been able to see a marabout, she'd still be alive."

For Zaina there is something miraculous about life. For me it tends to the absurd. The two positions meet up. Life only seems bearable to me when I am in love. At the moment I am not and so I have nothing on which to fall back. I find it impossible to conceal the first absurdity with a momentary fling.

Yesterday I said: " I have to leave you." It was short, no tears, no hitches. There were fruits piled in a basket. He squashed one in his palm as if to assess the improbable and the ambiguous opening up in him. We had only the night in common, the storms and our obsession with cities in ruins.

I was already in love, earlier, more intensely, even if there is no place for what I am looking. It was a big island. I was walking in fields of Barbary figs until evening. I was at the end of my strength, beyond exhaustion. I starved myself of him in order to better feel the embrace. Dawn, coming too soon, exposed the improbable boldness of our gestures.

" Why are you smiling?"

Zaina cannot understand how I can smile on the day I hear of someone's death. I would convince her of my sorrow if I pulled out my hair, bloodied my face or tore my dress. Do I even feel any sorrow? Dying is such a natural thing when it happens to others. I would feel threatened if it had been someone my own age. A misfortune that touches the older generation has little effect on me. So I can continue lounging in the sun. At four when it is time to close the window, I will think seriously about Aunt Régine's death.

The noises collide so gently behind the wall that I almost fall asleep. I hardly hear the doors slamming from one floor to another. The cries of women and children brush past me like confused whispers. Rivulets of sweat streak my neck. I ask Zaina to bring me a glass of iced water. She goes to the kitchen, dragging her espadrilles, and shadows move across the white wall. I hold the glass to each temple for a long time. The dream's contours are shot through with light stains that blur the image. Outside, a crimson sun pierces space like a ripe fruit about to fall into the dust of steps softened by desire. Tinkling anklets, fleeing lightly, scan the rhythm of clandestine loves just opening up in the falling light.

And then lovers will collapse in moist bedrooms, despite the now diminishing heat. How could it be snowing in my country right now? Has snow already fallen over there, and did I ever even have a country? Maybe I was dreaming. My eyes could have imagined those lakes and fields held in thick frost. Perhaps the car never did get stuck in the storm, and perhaps I was not the one who skidded on ice that night

in February. It could have happened somewhere else in a world in which I never set foot.

Zaina asks me which dress I will take on the
trip. I point to one at random. It does not really
matter, since my country seems not to exist in
my memory anymore. I will get off somewhere, wherever the plane lands, and look for
the coffin in a sleepy town. It will be made of
oak or maple, a hard wood that my fingers will
recognise by touch.

Zaina says that this dress will not be warm
enough for snow. I burst out laughing and
show her my sweat-covered skin. The hanger
holding the dress slips through my fingers. She
slowly backs away toward the door and runs to
the stairs.

She has plunged down the stairs. Now she
is in the courtyard telling the women that
Madame has lost her mind.

Constantine — Biskra, November 1970 —
April 1971.

Printed by
the workers of
Ateliers Graphiques Marc Veilleux Inc.
Cap-Saint-Ignace, Qué.

1638